The Questionable Ones

THE SWISS LIST

Judith Keller

THE QUESTIONABLE ONES

Translated by Tess Lewis

LONDON NEW YORK CALCUTTA

This publication has been supported by
a grant from the Goethe-Institut India.

swiss arts council
prohelvetia

This publication has been supported by
a grant from Pro Helvetia, Swiss Arts Council.

Seagull Books, 2022

Original published in German by Der gesunde Menschenversand, Luzern as
Die Fragwürdigen

© Der gesunde Menschenversand GmbH, Luzern, 2017

English translation © Tess Lewis, 2022

First published in English translation by Seagull Books, 2022

ISBN 978 1 80309 146 4

British Library Cataloguing-in-Publication Data
A catalogue record for this book is available from the British Library

Typeset by Seagull Books, Calcutta, India
Printed and bound in the USA by Integrated Books International

CONTENTS

BUCHEGGPLATZ

SCHWERT

MICAFIL

ELEKTROWATT

GLATT

WALDGARTEN

SUCCULENT COLLECTION

THE OTHER COW

Frau Hasler is walking along the street, not even with a dog. Crossing to the other side, she is run down by an escaping cow. Later she'll read that the cow saw what fate had in store for it and so it took measures. Not long after she was run over, the woman woke up in a hospital. Her red-cheeked son told her that the other cow had been permanently taken care of by five police officers, of which he was one. As for Frau Hasler, she lived on a few more years.

BUCHEGGPLATZ

ART

Patrick is an art student. On one of his pictures is written: *I love my parents*. Everyone thinks this is funny. But Patrick is serious.

LITERATURE

The boy came in and sat at the table. It was his favourite dinner, but he didn't say a word. After sticking a french fry into his mouth, he suddenly burst into tears. When his mother stroked his head, he buried his face in his arms and sobbed. His mother was not one to ask many questions, but we know that he was grieving for Winnetou, who had died on page 474.

FIVE WOMEN

Theodoa doesn't want any children, yet she's always expecting. Augustine would like everyone to miss her. Gudrun is continually getting into something. Claire is always said to be on her way. Veronique is a very promising woman. However, she doesn't know what her promise is. Not keeping something—that's her constant fear.

THE BROTHERS' VISITS

Once a year, one brother would visit the other. They both looked forward to it. When the brother was there, the two were annoyed that they could never think of anything to talk about. After three days, the brother would leave again. He would always write about a month later of how pleasant their time together had been. Until the next visit, they both believed the time they'd spent together had been pleasant. Then, for three days, they no longer believed it. Afterwards, they'd believe it again for almost an entire year. Only three days a year were they sure they didn't like each other.

BERNHARD

Bernhard thinks almost everything is bad.
When he does find something good, he feels
obliged to explain why to his surprised listeners.
In his explanation, he lists all that he finds bad
in comparison to what he finds good.
Meanwhile, a raw wind starts buffeting his heart
ever more wildly, and his list stretches on and
on. Bernhard is seen, increasingly, sitting on a
bench at a central tram stop. Now and again
previous listeners return. They take turns.

A MORAL TALE

With regard to Mrs Ochsenbein, she is
currently on vacation near a lake that mirrors
the surrounding mountains. Mrs Ochsenbein
has come up with a new variation on
encountering burglars. This is her new
method: at home, there are three wallets on her
kitchen table. Two are empty. In the third,
there are a few twenty-rappen coins. The
wallets surround a note which says: *Burglar,
this is all I have. The rest is in the bank*. And
when Mrs Ochsenbein explains her method to
the other hotel guests, she slyly adds that of
course there are a few hundred francs in the
apartment, namely, between pages 306 and 307
in her volume of *Green Henry*. At this the other
guests nod just as slyly. When Mrs Ochsenbein
returns home from vacation two weeks later,
she finds the lock on her door broken. Yet the
apartment is neat and the bills are still in *Green
Henry*. The note is on the kitchen table. Under

her lines, an unfamiliar hand has written: *Fair enough*. Since then Mrs Ochsenbein has been tormented by a guilty conscience, and as far as slyness goes, she has given it up completely.

RELATIONSHIP

A man wishes that the woman he's with would knock him out. Because she won't, he can only appreciate her. The fact that he can only appreciate her and that she won't knock him out fills him with a complicated sense of guilt, which he tries to put into words on long Sunday afternoons. She, however, would much rather be appreciated by him than knock him out. They aren't quite on the same wavelength.

FREDDY OR MAXIMILIAN

A man named Freddy or Maximilian always took views that those around him at any given time did not share. He wasn't sure if the views he took were sound, but with his eloquence, he could convince everyone. And even though he wasn't sure his views were sound, those around him suddenly were. He would then let himself be convinced by them. But what others said never completely convinced him. As a result, he was never convinced of himself either.

THE SON-IN-LAW

The family of the newly married bride expects their son-in-law to behave as members of family expect. But he wants to behave in ways his in-laws don't expect in order to train them not to expect anything of him. He does this because he doesn't want to disappoint his in-laws under any circumstances.

FOR ALL I CARE

He wanted to leave her. She said, 'For all I care.' It all depended on how much she cared. But he couldn't leave for all she cared. A strange, unfathomable terrain lay before him. For all she cared, he only ever found his way back to her. And for all he cared, it didn't work.

IN PRINCIPLE

Ferdinand only meets women who, in principle, want him.

XAVIER

Xavier always falls in love with women he doesn't like. He never notices this while he's in love. But he does see it afterwards.

ANTICIPATION

Muriel is one of those women others prefer to think back on than deal with directly in real time. Thus everyone is grateful for the memories they will have of her and so leave her with a certain sense of anticipation.

TRUST

She believes him when he tells her he's lying.
He believes her when she tells him she's lying.
That will do.

FIDELITY

In being true to him, she's afraid she's not being true to herself. She doesn't know if she'd like to be true to herself. So it's not clear to her to whom then she should be true.

LETTING YOURSELF GO

Although people are always telling Frau
Gantenbein that she's really letting herself go,
she has never, as long as she can remember,
ever let herself go. And now she's too old.

USEFULNESS

Instead of living with him, she now lives with her heartache. It's almost the same thing. When she could use him, he's not there.

ALFONSO

Alfonso can finally be a wreck. Before he was rock.

RÜDIGER

Rüdiger has no idea what to do with himself.
Any suggestions?

GERALDINE

Everything looks familiar to Geraldine. That's why she can't find her car.

ALBERTA

For a long time, Alberta was solitary. But now she's solo.

JOSEPHINE

Josephine is not all there. That's important to her.

HIGH TIME

This afternoon, a far-fetched woman is crossing a vast, brightly shining gravel-covered lot, at the far end of which tiny people are pottering about in flower beds. Behind them rises a gleaming housing development that looks like it landed there. The air is saturated with rain; the first drops have fallen and disappeared into the meadow. The sky is blue and grey and dense, and it's as if the development were illuminating the sun, which shimmers far away in the sky like a silverfish. The development gleams silvery dark green in front of the forest and it swallows all sounds, even those of the children, who are carrying heavy shopping bags home to their apartments, past the ducks swimming wildly back and forth in the elevated decorative fountain. Behind it, there it stands, the distribution substation, just before the forest. She has been waiting for it to be high time for a good while now.

SCHWERT

IN A HOUSE

A band of light lay on a hillside as if a glance from
half-closed eyes had fallen from above. On the hill
stood a house and in it lived a man whose
movements were slow. He slowly raked the
leaves. He had a wife and two sons. His wife
looked like an owl with her brown and golden
eyes. She had taken to standing behind herself and
sending her body on ahead and calmly watching
what happened to it. Their marriage was a muted
one. The daily hurts and stings they caused each
other through minor misunderstandings made
them aware of the beautiful, skittish love they had
for each other. She took care of him. That care lay
in faint wrinkles around her mouth. She could
only treat him seriously and solemnly. It's true
that her solemnity gave rise to an inhibition,
which made him feel sheltered. When he entered
the church he loved, he had the sense that God
was looking at him like a not entirely successful
experiment. A brazen, exuberant feeling trickled
through him when he caressed his wife in church,
brushing his fingertips along her forearm and her

thigh during the sermon, before God. He reddened and lowered his eyes; laughter trembled in his throat; he shook himself, saw Jesus on the cross—caught the scent of his wife's soft cheeks, which smelled good. The two sons went their way inconspicuously. The mother spoke to her children in a tone that made every request and every worry seem like a secret that made them allies. The younger of the sons had flat, wing-like arms and in his dreams, he tried to circle above the house in flight. The older one sometimes didn't know why he was alive and his mother stroked his hair and, smiling, whispered in his ear, 'You are here because God thought you here.' On Sundays, he helped the priest pass the wine and, kneeling, rang the little bells. He liked the air in the church, the sound of footsteps, and the sense of his smallness, which lost all danger and became solemn. The two sons had already moved out without a sound when their father fell ill. It cost him great effort to move. He often contemplated the snails in the dirt of the garden. Occasionally, fear coursed through him, and he would flinch in alarm. He held his wife's hand. She spoke softly to him, which blanketed his fear, but underneath, he could feel it throb.

BREAKING IT TO HIM

She called her father. His voice told her that he wasn't reachable, she should try again later. She called again. His voice told her that he wasn't reachable, she should try again later. She called again, and again his voice told her that she should try again later. Her father had died suddenly a few days earlier. The daughter had the sense that he hadn't understood. She wanted to break it to him slowly.

MEMORY

Sometimes she thinks she sees him from a distance. She almost follows him. But then she remembers: he's already much farther away.

MISSING

She misses him. She can't do anything about it. But he is missed. While there's nothing she can do, he can be missed. But she has to be there because he can't be missed without her. She's there so he can be missed. It's the only thing he can still do.

TIME

After he died, she felt that his time could no longer run out. Now it still counted.

MISSION

Mrs Vogelsanger was not pleased when a lovely
word occurred to her. Then it occurred to her
that there were, indeed, lovely words. In the
last few years she had become smaller and had
withdrawn into a small part of her body. When
she walked, she seemed to lose ground, that is,
to go backwards, even though she was going
forwards. Recently, in the middle of the night,
she was given a mission. She got out of bed,
put her clothes on, and limped downstairs
slowly and furtively. She greeted the surprised
cleaning lady, opened the heavy door, and—
the sky was still almost completely dark—went
to the train station. 'Last night, I fulfilled a
mission,' she said that afternoon to a trembling
woman sitting in the cafeteria and waiting. She
positioned her sentences so that they were
clearly visible in the air and looked up at them
from below, always speaking rather
triumphantly. She tensely scrutinized her

listeners' reactions for the meaning her sentences acquired. 'I took the train for the mission,' she said and waited to see how the expression on the quivering woman's face would change with this information. 'You only dreamed of the mission,' a thin voice said. It was the voice of another woman also sitting in the cafeteria, who had sharp ears. Mrs Vogelsanger became dejected. She slowly made her way back to her room, supporting herself on the wall the entire way. She sat down, exhausted, on the edge of her bed. When she took off her wool jacket, she noticed the ticket that proved she had taken the train at 4:30 that morning. She wanted to keep the ticket and laid it carefully in the waste basket.

MRS SÄGISSER

Mrs Sägisser wants to go help her parents make hay. When the weather is fine, she wants to hurry. The sliding doors open. Cars slowly drive past. A younger woman, who looks familiar, stands next to her and asks, 'Wouldn't it be nicer if you visited your parents tomorrow?' Behind the cars is the church, and behind it is the hill on which her parents live, and between the hill and the church is the cemetery where her parents lie. Mrs Sägisser draws back, the sliding doors open behind her, she steps into the elevator, enters a room, Mrs Züger lies in bed, asleep; in her sleep her mouth has shifted—a crevice in the middle of her face—she snores, the television is on, the church bells ring, the heat, the hay, the hill, the hay, what about the hay, Mrs Sägisser gropes her way to her room, looks out the window, the weather is beautiful, she's filled with relief, she no longer knows why.

HIGH TIME

Tonight, a far-fetched woman is walking through the city. The air is warm and saturated with rain, and in the direction from which the evening sun had earlier thrown a sharp rectangle onto the houses, she senses someone looking at her. Empty tramcars with open doors stand, unlit, at the stations. The drivers stand next to trams, talking at them as they smoke. People in sombreros are also waiting, and gradually the night mosquitos arrive. Dark water streams from the ground, and a truck crosses the bridge. Before long the far-fetched woman passes single-family homes, catalpas and their scent. She feels she's being watched by a glowing pink head, sticking out from under the room's heavy curtains, which is also a lamp gazing out into the night. The terrain is stepped with trees and garbage bins, mosquitos and flowers, and as she walks down a long street, she notices on a staircase below her a fox that stops when she does. Behind it stretches the valley, filled with shimmering lights. When she turns away, so does the fox, or, when the fox turns away, so does she. She doesn't look back, walks past the bundles of cardboard boxes, through the thick undergrowth, and leaves the rain-covered plates and the glass takeaway table they're lying on where they are and follows the arrows. At Schwert Station, she stops. It's drizzling, and there are night mosquitos. She drinks white wine and eats braided bread. She listens. She has been waiting for it to be high time for a good while now.

MICAFIL

PARAGRAPHS

Last night the paragraphs appeared in her room again. They advanced through the darkness, stood at the side of her bed for a long time, letting their gaze rest on her. Their feathers rustled softly in a draught of air. She sat up and opened the window. 'Off with you,' she said, and a fluttering motion spread through the paragraphs. They left the badly heated room indistinctly and went into the forest. The next morning, once again, there was no letter in the mailbox.

CASTING

A police car drives slowly along the streetcar tracks in front of the central station. The officers scrutinize the waiting pedestrians through the window. Most of those waiting here are out of the question. But some do come into question. These are the questionable ones.

EXTRATERRESTRIAL

It's impossible to cross this desert. It's impossible to climb this fence. It's impossible to cross this sea in a rubber boat. Those who saw him coming were blinded. From far away, he had shone like a never-before-seen star. But when he reaches shore, he's one of the ones wearing a gold space blanket. The people on the beach can't believe he's still alive and greet him a bit incredulously, like an extraterrestrial. The farther away from the shore, the less they believe he was ever in danger, because if he really could have died, then he would have. It's not at all possible that he's still alive. And anyone who's not alive is impossible.

NO PAPERS

A few years ago, Esperance fled over the sea in a boat. She didn't drown, but now she lives underground.

WAR

He declares war on them. They don't
understand him. He declares war on them.
They don't understand him. He tries one more
time. They don't understand him. Because he
can't explain it, he has to return to the war.
There's no time to waste. There's only one seat
left on the plane.

A LITTLE RELATIONSHIP ADVICE

Emil now works at the airport. Dogs sniff the
suitcases. Emil's heart beats more quickly when
the dogs start barking. 'Today I caught another
drug mule,' he tells his friends in the evening
and leans back in his chair. Ever since Emil has
been corralling drug mules, others have
noticed that he's alert and indefatigable. His
wife hopes that the stream of drugs won't run
dry. Emil brings her perfume bottles and nail
clippers that the passengers have to leave
behind at security. Every night he brings her
something. Before it was different. Gifts liven
up a relationship: keep this in mind.

KONI

Even before the electricity bill came, Koni was sure he had to be careful. Now that the bill lay before him, the connection of the state to his cat's disappearance was clear. With a languid gesture, he lit the bill on fire and threw it in the stairwell, where it soon went out. He would have liked to call out for help, but all indications were that everyone was involved. When Koni saw the cat sitting in front of his door the next morning, he couldn't trust it any more. He ignored its meows, tears ran down his face.

MARTHA

Since the business has stopped making a profit, Martha's absence is needed. Her job now consists of being absent. It's work that takes a strong will and persistence as well as a mastery of the relevant invisibility. This becomes clear after a few days. Martha is so poorly paid for this work that she can only absent herself badly. Absently, she smashes the collected bottles on the ground. The shards of glass that glitter like distant stars under the streetlamps light up the way. She hears the steps of confederates as if from very far away. They're coming from the shards or from even farther away. Soon, they arrive.

BETTER DAYS

Leaves sail down the street, whirling a little, a
branch nods: these and similar things occur,
but all on their own. Ever since he can
remember, Anton has been sitting heavily on a
chair by the window. On top of it all, an
important woman has not written back for
days. But in this instant, when a cloud suddenly
passed passes before the sun, he sees something
he has never seen before: airy creatures off in
the distance as if these were better days. Will
they disappear the moment they feel his eyes
on them? Anton stays calm. They move
fluffily, airily, but only barely. They browse. As
they graze, their bright fur rises and falls.
Something like glittering screens rise around
them, and they linger in the screens' shade.
What's behind them is visible through their
fur, and yet the slight movements of the
screens, now swaying slightly in the wind, are
apparent on them. Anton senses that the

animals can feel his gaze, but they are still pondering, heads lowered, looking at the grass. How can they get out of grazing? How can they get near the gleaming screens? With verve? Announced or by surprise? And how can they rise with the screens? It won't be an easy undertaking, the animals realize, as does Anton. Must they wait for a particular wind, a certain light? And then, will they find Anton on his chair or will they get lost on the long journey through time? Anton can see these questions shining through the creatures. He wants to help them. He whispers fiercely, 'Patience. Don't be afraid. I'll wave to you. Keep watch for me, and I'll do what I can.'

CECILIA AND HER FRIENDS

A group of unkempt people are sitting at the table. They're friends. It's already late; they can tell from the reflections in the window, in which one woman spots herself like a discarded sketch. They can tell by the feeling that their brains have shifted slightly because of the wine they'd started drinking when the half fir tree was still visible through the window in the twilight. The tree's missing top left a clear view of a window behind which first a woman ran past, then a man, as if they had to divide up time. Maybe they were having an argument, but not much could be heard.

The woman, who lives on the third floor where the friends are gathered around the table, sometimes notices that she lets a lot of things happen, but nothing ever happens to her. Those who always want to come over have become her friends. Every evening they sit around the green metal garden table in her living room and talk. When a glass is put down on the table, it makes a clanking sound. The woman these people gather around is called Cecilia. She welcomes her friends every evening with a friendly, desperate smile to which they've grown accustomed. There are breadcrumbs on the table, along with cheese rinds and the foamy ashes of many cigarettes; the friends are in the habit of dining here every night. Anyone who looks into the others' faces at a late hour sees their features far away through the smoke. The friends turn their innermost parts outward and talk about their fears and what they've observed about themselves. They often speak in astonished tones. Every evening they empty several bottles of wine from the corner store; no one ever gets seriously drunk. To Cecilia, it all appears very far away, and she watches herself and her friends like cyclists lost on meadow paths.

She's not sure she wants to hear everything her friends say. When not talking about themselves, they tend to analyse Cecilia and tell her how she is. They don't believe Cecilia is in a position to free herself on her own. Cecilia nods sweetly and pulls out a cigarette with her slender fingers. She encourages those who are speaking with approving nods because it's good to talk late into the night and to push further back those days on which night advances like the imperceptibly shifting fir trees at the forest's edge. Besides, everything she hears about herself seems clear to her. She now hears a languid voice saying that the speaker is afraid to walk past a group of people unless they have a few tired dogs with them. Cecilia nods because she would like to support everything that is expressed. What gets into a sentence seems comprehensible. Only later does she ask herself if she's the one who said the sentence, but she probably wasn't. Cecilia's friends enjoy her approval and that may be a reason they come. They always come as a group. If they came alone, they would feel trapped by Cecilia's shyness and would sit there mutely. When Cecilia talks about herself, she has the impression she's merely maintaining something, even when she tries to pull something out of herself so that afterwards it won't be there any more.

She says in an astonished voice: 'Before, a tree's beauty moved me to tears but now I seem to be dried out; nothing touches me any more.' Moreover, she always seems to be nodding. Her head sways slightly as if it were shakily trying to keep its balance on her neck. Some of the approval others have experienced from her could perhaps be attributed to this particular physical trait.

The door to the living room opens quietly, and suddenly a little curly haired person who can't sleep appears in the doorway. Confident she's not interrupting, she scampers over to Cecilia on thin, little legs. Cecilia is alarmed at the late hour and the clouds of smoke through which she notices her daughter only after some time. She feels ashamed because she senses her friends think she has no authority but is ruled by her daughter, just as she herself has always thought. She strokes her young daughter's head and tells her in a friendly voice to go back to bed. But the girl pulls on Cecilia's leg and pushes her cheek out with her tongue. Cecilia can see her friends looking askance at her. Cecilia summons all her courage and says, 'I remember, as a child, also feeling that having to sleep at night was a humiliation.' The friends hear her high, helpless voice, which Cecilia also notices as soon as she hears herself through her friends' ears. The friends are hoping the child will be considerate and recognize the barbarity of robbing her mother of this moment of freedom and intimacy. Does the child, with her large eyes, not see the tears of shame above her mother's friendly smile? The friends now intervene and start shooing the child away in Cecilia's stead. Once again, they've taken something out of Cecilia's hands. She is only just able to see it, before she understands again.

The process takes a long time. Many pedagogical pronouncements are made; the friends' voices harden until a thin man who is covered in hair comes up from downstairs. He greets no one and resolutely picks up the small, now screaming daughter, and carries her to her bed in the dark room with glowing stars on the ceiling, which at night seem to be harbouring rather pointed plans. He will tell her she must sleep and then he will leave the room. Cecilia will be stricken with embarrassment, which will bloom heatedly over her face. At the same time, she envies the thin man his power. In the living room, the mood has become strange. The friends are not fond of the thin man and for good reasons, which are now laid out on the table. They blame him for Cecilia's state. 'Do you have even a shred of pride?' she is asked. When he comes upstairs again to make himself a snack, one of the friends asks him why he's with Cecilia when he obviously looks down on her. The thin man with the long face says with a sneer that only people who haven't done anything with their lives ask questions like that. The question fills the early morning hours. Anyone listening closely is aware of the first birds and sees a branch sway on the fir tree. The friends discuss how Cecilia can be helped. Meanwhile, Cecilia studies her grimacing face in the wine and worries that her reflection has recognized her. The friends are certain that Cecilia must leave the thin man with the tattoos. Cecilia's mouth wears a friendly smile as she listens to them. She understands everything and, behind her lowered eyelids, collects all the fluid helplessness flowing inexorably into her.

Dawn has broken and the half fir tree is visible again. The friends are still there, but their sentences have grown sparse. The first heads are sinking onto the tabletop. Others stretch out on the sofa or directly on the floor. The friends are everywhere, breathing deeply. Cecilia stands still for a long time and listens. Then she steps quietly over the sleeping bodies and slips downstairs and out of the house. The early morning air greets Cecilia as if it had been waiting for her for a long time. She shivers, but nothing seems easier than to go, now, walking along the street with long steps, walking on and on, out of the city, past the gas station towards the wintery horizon that is rising like a bright line over the houses, it even turns slowly and clearly towards her, so that now she is walking directly towards it, towards the horizon—and yet her legs have turned off into a side street and entered the first open bakery. Cecilia only wants to buy one roll, but her hoarse voice has plotted against her. She buys several.

Tonight, a far-fetched woman is walking along
the trolley wires in the direction in which the
evening has receded, red, behind the buildings.
'No feeding' reads a sign propped up against a
tree trunk. It occurs to her that she would like
to walk through the city making the gesture of
strewing grains. Birds would come, as would
Julius Baer, whose gleaming office complex she
is just passing. If the buildings were animals,
they would be the kind with scruffy skins but
his would be like that of a shiny eel. On the
roofs of the buildings, floors that do not yet
exist are placed on fine rods. She passes
excavators and red and white safety barriers.
She finds rest at Micafil. The sun has set and
Jesus looks down at her from a billboard and
says, 'Fork everything up and be forked up by
everything.' But what is there? Birds and
gasoline, a gospel centre and Rohrmax
plumbers who are there for you twenty-four

hours. Then what? What happens after twenty-four hours? Tiny, almost stationary mosquitos have emerged from the growth entwined around the tram stop sign. She stands up abruptly and walks down a dark, almost empty main road. Everything is dark and takes its course. She can hear the river and a few ducks dreaming. There are very few people. But then, under enormous spotlights giving off a strong, bluish light, men with gelled hair and tight jeans suddenly appear. They're carrying water guns with which they spray the finish on their cars, oblivious to everything around them. Above them, on the fifth floor of a run-down office building, Julius Baer stands in an enormous brown fur with a lightly averted smile enveloped in Latin music blaring from a car. He gazes over it all but says nothing. The woman walks quickly through the night, now following the river. She has been waiting for it to be high time for a good while now.

ELEKTROWATT

THE SECOND CELLAR

Roswitha had a second cellar built. She offered
the construction workers a beer and showed
them the clay cat she had painted red with
white dots. The cat stood under a cactus on the
second floor to which a curving staircase led.
There was very little room on the steps for the
workers' feet, stacks of newspapers and piles of
cardboard boxes had stood along the walls for
years. This was a large house with a view of the
lake which altered every day but on this day it
looked like a light grey wall, which didn't seem
threatening, at most somewhat unsettling after
too many cups of coffee. The other shore
looked like something towering over a wall.
But it didn't incite any curiosity, the viewer
soon had enough. Roswitha noticed the
workers' embarrassment as she led them to the
cat. It reminded her of something, but she
couldn't figure out what and she thought she
heard one of the workers softly call 'pitié!' This

amused her, but there was no longer a way back
and the workers stood around the clay cat and
admired it while Roswitha twitched with
suppressed laughter. On some days the lake
resembled a forgotten, pale blue silk scarf. After
a storm it was green-grey and wrinkled. In
other words, depending on the weather, the lake
looked younger or older and occasionally
Roswitha, who was never sure how she should
feel, would take the lake's humours as a
suggestion for the day's mood. In the new
cellar, she stored the garden chairs she had
bought forty years before, heavy, old radiators,
Velcro fasteners, old rubber bands, old
shoelaces, three broken sewing machines, bags,
and razors her husband had left behind when he
moved out four months earlier. They had
bought the radiators for her first apartment.
Light had broken into the apartment from all
sides as if through poorly sewn fabric. Roswitha
saw the dust whirling out of his hair when he
ran his hand through it to please her. She wrote
sent letters to the places where he was pursuing
advanced training. She confused 'l's and 's's and
wrote 'I song for you,' which pleased him at

first since he was a composer. But later, as if to offer an all-encompassing explanation to the lawyers, he said with exasperation, 'She can't even get her 'l's and 's's right,' and he showed them the letter as proof. Why 'not even'? There was no longer an opportunity for her to ask him because she had the feeling that she was a boat and, whenever she got near him, was driving him away like a wave. 'You're robbing me, you're stealing from me, right in front of my eyes,' Roswitha said to her daughter who at this moment came creeping out of the second cellar with an armful of empty plastic bags. The daughter lowered her arms and the bags rustled softly as they slipped to the ground. Roswitha's daughter stroked her mother's broad, firm back. She took her mother's hands. Together they returned the bags to the new second cellar. They climbed the stairs, carefully placing their feet where there was still room.

AMBITION

She wanted to do things well, but she found
she couldn't. 'I accept the fact that I can't do
everything well,' she said, but she didn't really.
She wrote a suicide note. In her opinion, it
wasn't very good. It's only thanks to her
ambition that she's still alive—her suicide
notes were never good enough.

MRS MÄRZ

With an ink eraser, Mrs März removes the mistakes in the third graders' dictations. The parents are delighted with their children's progress. The parent teacher conferences are cheerful, the children's aptitude is reflected in each dictation assignment. Mrs März will soon lose her position. The cause is a suspicious father who had his child repeat the same dictation and found twenty mistakes. Mrs März will tell many people, 'I wanted to sow confidence in order to harvest it later.' Because of her sweet voice, everyone had actually already had complete confidence in Mrs März.

REGARDING ANIMALS

'As for animals,' Gregor said, 'I just want to
say that after my dog charges cyclists, barking
and baring his teeth, he lies on his back behind
the hedge, laughing at the faces they make.
Loud, clearly, and without restraint.'

THE UNIVERSE

She tries to get interested in something. But whenever she gets interested in something, she has to think of the universe.

WORK

Anatol was out of work. Now he goes out looking for work. It walks impassively through the days, and he follows behind. It talks to him but is hard to understand. It's as if he had to overtake it in order to understand what it's saying. But he always has to follow it. He doesn't want to lose it. However sometimes he's too slow and it disappears from his field of vision and he trips. 'Where'd you go for so long?' people with long beards ask him. 'I was looking for work,' he says. They nod.

EMILY

Ever since Emily stopped taking everything
personally, she has been doing well. But not
personally.

ODYSSEUS

This is not for me, Odysseus thinks when he's travelling, looking around at what there is out in the world. He has used his vacations to ascertain what is not for him. He wants to believe, eventually, that what he has is for him.

HOLDING HER OWN

Helen held her own very well in her new position. She held her own well in the next months too, especially in June and July. From August on, she no longer held her own quite as well. At some point, she held her own so forcefully that people noticed.

TWO FRIENDS

On the lakeshore, the people in the tram now crossing the bridge see a man who has a good friend. The two friends stand in the soft glow of a night lantern. It's a mild night, in which many things could happen. If the people had coats of fur, the hairs would be standing on end but not out of fear. It would be from excitement, from being part of the mosquitos' and moths' celebration and their frenzied dance around the streetlamps. The man leans on his friend, his legs and upper body at a diagonal in the air, his forehead pressed against that of his friend. The two men's weight is drawn together at this point. They speak to each other, swearing an oath, mouth to mouth and next to them lies the dark lake. There are even darker spots in it; where the boats would be there are now black holes. It's known, now, where they are, should it come to that someday. It will be possible to enter the future through these spots. Or the future will penetrate the present through them. It must be an intimate conversation between these two good friends on this night at the lakeshore. Little time has passed but the friend is suddenly in the man's shadow, thrown by an illuminated wall that reflects the passing tram without understanding that one must take the friends wherever they appear at any moment.

HIGH TIME

This afternoon, a woman who has always felt herself to be far-fetched walks along the lakeshore. A sun reigns who means everything personally, as do the swans who are searching for something. A large mirror hangs in the glassy second story of a white villa and in front of it is an empty leather chair. The woman passes the blue boats, everything is laden with sun, but nothing is of use. The woman takes a rest at the Elektrowatt stop. The people exiting through the sliding door appear as if seen from above. A man wearing a suit climbs, well-fed, over and above them and disappears. There is a rustling from the quay. Where are the swans? They're looking for something in their feathers. They won't find it here, nor in their feathers. A hedge trembles in the wind and the light and there are three arrows on the ground. These you can follow. It's time to go and steal the mirror. At night the swans will come and snap at the flags. They're looking for a high time. It's difficult to find here. It's all the higher.

GLATT

A BLEAK BEGINNING

At this very moment, Marie develops—why will forever remain a bit of a mystery—an intense fear of dirt. Marie is in a train. She should get out at this stop but can't bring herself to touch the button on the door. She stands motionless in front of the button. She's not able to push it at the next station either, nor at the one after. More stations pass, distant names on the station signs. Marie simply can't bring herself to touch the button. The train is empty. Marie travels from station to station. She can't get out. Marie travels to the train depot. A kind train conductor frees her. Thirty trains are lined up next to each other as in an enormous stall. They are completely still. Marie looks at them for a long time as darkness falls. After hours of waiting, her uncomprehending parents come and collect her. Marie's future inability to explain her reaction to them has its bleak beginning here in the nightly train depot.

MONEY

She says that her wallet was stolen and she needs a train ticket. Everyone knows she needs heroin. She knows that the others know this. She knows it and says, 'My wallet was just stolen, could you give me 10,000 francs?' She wants to help them misunderstand her. They have never understood that a heroin addict doesn't need money.

MIRJA

Mirja had a young son. She'd have liked to switch him off from now and again. Unfortunately, that wasn't possible, and she grew more and more tired day after day. She said to herself, 'You either have children or you don't.' She said, 'Children aren't like televisions that you can switch on and off.' She said, 'What's nice about children is that they have a will of their own.' She said all this and even believed it. And yet, one day she disconnected her son. Where? In a busy train station. This was proven to her later thanks to surveillance cameras. She could scarcely believe it herself.

ALBERTINE

They say that Albertine feels very well supported in her relationship, at work, in her apartment. Without her ever having heard this said, the moments when she feels supported increase. Suddenly she looks down at the ground, far below her. Despite her efforts, she can't reach it, she's so well supported. She's awake while sleeping. Sleep lies below her like a dark river. In the middle of the day, she has a fear of heights. It's evident when you look at her. Someone lays a calming hand on her shoulder. She's grateful. She is surrounded by good people, all at a loss.

POTENTIAL

People say that Josephine remains far below her potential. Even she notices how she tilts back her head. There it is—my potential, she thinks looking up at the scaffolding that extends metallically in all directions. Far below, Josephine can hear the wind shake it. She calls out, 'Come down, potential, I'd like to stay with you a while, I'm with you, I'm part of you.'

THE ANNOUNCEMENT

One evening, Mrs Finsterwald prepares a special dinner. She has an announcement to make to her family. 'I have an announcement to make,' she says, first looking down at her plate, then into her daughter's eyes, then into her son's eyes, and finally into the eyes of her husband. 'We'll have to find a solution. I'm sure we can.' She gives each of them a long look, her husband, her son, her daughter. Then she gets up from the table. 'I knew we were a strong family.' She leaves the dining room to give her long-suppressed emotion free rein. She'd like to jump for joy. She's forgotten that she hasn't yet made her announcement. She'll remember soon; that's not a sight we'd like to see—quick, let's leave!

DID MRS SIEGENTALER
HELP THE NEEDY?

The cold has settled into the faces of the
houses; passers-by are bitterly sized up. Mrs
Siegentaler sees a broad, staggering man fall.
He rubs his elbows and glances around. That
urge to confirm that what just happened really
did is familiar to Mrs Siegentaler. She likes to
consider herself someone who saves others and
imagines herself taking care of the man. In the
garage, along with him, there would be others,
addicts and those who are needy, who have
fallen down or are wounded. In her conscience,
she talked to and gently stroked heads
deformed by fate. 'The right way is dependent
on you,' she'd say, and solace would settle in
the eyes of the afflicted. But when the man
reveals himself to be a drunkard asking for a
franc, she gives him nothing. Nevertheless, he
bows politely as if he had been a recipient of
her compassion. Mrs Siegentaler is confused—

has she helped this needy man out of his distress and communicated hope's warmth? 'You can't help everyone,' she whispers, 'and because in my life I am desperately concerned about consequences, I may not help you.' When she looks up, the bearded man has disappeared. At home in her cellar, there are no needy people. When she looks out the window, Mrs Siegentaler sees the bearded man standing like a tree in her garden. It's almost dark and a heavy snow is falling. 'A new day will come,' Mrs Siegentaler thinks, 'and it will bring clarity and relief.'

A LONG NIGHT

Next to the folding bed stood a real bed. On it, mouth slightly open, lay the daughter, her hair now also turned grey, who had come yesterday evening, solemn, heartsore, and dutiful, at her mother's behest.

On the telephone, the latter had said in a rattling voice, 'I'm almost certain that I'll die tonight. If you'd like to be with me, please come and spend the night here. And please don't forget that I've turned yellow and my head wobbles as if I were constantly nodding.'

The grey-haired daughter came to the nursing home, in which her yellow, shrunken mother had rented a lovely apartment. From carefully kept plates, they ate slices of buttered bread that the trembling mother had determinedly and impatiently cut with a dull knife and of which she only ate one. They drank rosehip tea with sugar, and the mother's nodding head seemed to agree.

That night, already long after just two hours, the daughter spoke encouragingly to her mother. At some point the mother said into her daughter's murmured words that she couldn't die because poisonous ants were working on her back and her leg. And besides she needed to go to the toilet, a long, laborious path that led her first through an open door and then past a small, cream-coloured canapé, behind which she had to take a sharp left turn, catching a glimpse, ahead on the right, of the round dining table and the little kitchen, both rather ghostly in the dim light. 'Would you be so kind as to help me?'

The daughter, still agile and lively despite her age, suffering only an occasional sharp twinge in her neck, offered her mother as a support the crook formed between her elbow and her hand braced on her hip. The mother's back was nearly bent double with age so that she often saw her feet when she walked. For a long time—was it hours?—they travelled in this way through the tiny apartment. It was an arduous journey, and little light came from the bedroom. The mother's feet moved along the floor like two slow ships and the daughter was suddenly struck with spasmodic stomach cramps. They'd finally reached the bathroom and closed the door behind them. The daughter reacted to the intimate proximity with composure but still she suddenly had to vomit into the bathtub. This inspired her mother, who was well over ninety and had just sat down on the toilet, to stand up unassisted and stroke her elderly daughter's back, which was trembling from exhaustion, nausea, and the will to do everything right. Enlivened by her own consoling, she guided her suddenly haggard daughter with her slow, ship-like steps back through the peculiar land of her apartment. Her daughter seemed to her very old, she herself felt alert and lucid. She heard each sound with exceptional clarity. All the objects seemed directed towards her with a mysterious tone. During the night, their bodies seemed to have become strangely dense and at the same time frayed as if they had grown fur. She heard the refrigerator's hum as an earnest song. Where an armchair once stood, there now sat a dark, sleeping animal. She heard it breathe deeply and listened to it reverently.

The apartment's cleanness hung heavily in the air: the dishes in the dishwasher must already have dried, in the refrigerator all the food was neatly packed, and in the window, outside of which large trees stood in daytime, the mother saw two faintly blurry, yellow figures joined at the arms. She slowly approached the distant figures that grew ever larger in the window, and when she got right up close, the yellow figures lost their colour in the night that streamed in and over them through the window. She herself merged with the window and looked out into the night where the trees stood, rustling. She briefly found herself in one of the trees, felt the night wind, and glanced back from the tree at the dark window. She saw herself in the smaller, more bent of the two figures in nightgowns. She felt calm and waved imperceptibly to herself, then left the ants to the tree.

How much time had passed before they walked by the little canapé, the small oval table, the vases and newspapers that weakly emitted their nocturnal light, the dark sleeping, breathing animal? They were almost astonished when they finally reached the bedroom again. The mother convinced her daughter to sleep in the large, comfortable bed while she stretched out on the folding bed. Whereas her daughter, rocked by nausea, tossed back and forth throughout the long night, the old woman spoke soothingly to her daughter as if she'd never forgotten a word and hadn't taken some delight, even if tinged with suspicion, at pronouncing every word only as 'ee', which granted her for a few hours, as she lay alone and lonely in bed, a gleaming, effortless understanding with everyone.

But the daughter did not feel calmed by her mother's encouraging words. She asked, 'Wouldn't you like to go to sleep and die a discreet, redeeming death as you'd planned?' The mother confirmed that she would like to do just that, but at the moment her back was itching like crazy again and keeping her awake even though she was beyond exhausted and wanted nothing more than to finally look back over her long and probably fulfilled life from that vantage. At that very moment, she felt the scorching ants working away poisonously and invisibly at her back and knees and became enraged and impatient. She tried bitterly to ask God, with whom she frequently spoke, in a reasonable way why he had given her the holy feeling that she would die that night. But even as she thought about it, she again failed to come up with all the words and the pain drained away the patience to wait for them. Her bad leg hurt, and all the listlessness that had kept her from getting out of bed, leaving the house, and hearing what was going on in the world over the last few days returned. She read the newspaper headlines only with scorn; she was no longer concerned about war and misery; in the last few months, she had dismissed the world like a wayward but adult child. The nausea-racked daughter said, 'You can go in peace. You don't need to feel obligated to live longer on our account even though we'll all miss you. You'll sit up in heaven on a cloud, swinging your healthy legs. We'll dress you exactly as you want to be dressed, in this beautiful wool jacket, and we'll bury you in the grave you've chosen for yourself. You can let go, you can now let that life clinging so tightly to you go without worry on this night that is still not completely over. Let it go, chase that life away! If you can't fall asleep now, which is perfectly normal, by the way, then take a third or even two-thirds of this sleeping pill. That's certainly permitted, considering your difficult situation.'

But the mother, suddenly in command of her words again, said, 'I don't want to take any more sleeping pills because then I'll start seeing things. I don't want to be delirious when I meet my death or I'll assume I'm just imagining it. Besides, I have the impression that the otherwise very nice staff in this nursing home has wanted to get me hooked on sleeping pills and medicine in the last few weeks. So I deliberately never took any of the medicine, wanting to choke off any creeping addiction right from the start. On top of that, you know that they're earning ever more money off old people's crooked backs. I recently even dreamed that a new ointment was being palmed off on me and I had to listen the whole time to how it was going to help me even though I was much too tired to pay attention.

The more medications I take, the more the doctors laugh up their sleeves. That's why I wouldn't let them operate on me either. I'd rather suffer this itching than an ultimately unverifiable but still previously existent addiction.'

The daughter, in the meantime, had had to vomit again. How late was it anyway? She felt ancient, her limbs were heavy, something indescribably mute in the flowers printed on the wallpaper permeated the incipient morning.

The trees outside the window were still vague, black tangles standing on their own. The two women lay restless, lonely and dissatisfied in their beds. Time, pass already!

When morning came, the daughter woke unrested and dismayed. Her mother was still alive. She was alive and had hardly forgotten the entire night, only the last two hours had she experienced a superficial, blathering dream. The mother and the daughter both had headaches. There was a knock on the door. A nurse brought coffee. She entered the room like life itself and did the objects in it some good. That night, the daughter had had to experience being switched with her mother. But you good, grey daylight! Now everything was very earthly. At some point the daughter went back to her house. She called a few people and told each of them that her mother was still alive. While she said it, she sounded confused. Those she called didn't know what to do with the information. Their words of sympathy and the appropriate feelings they had prepared now seemed shamelessly premature. The daughter lay down in her own bed. It was noon, the sun had come out, and she tried to sleep. Was she going to die now? She felt extremely exhausted. In the nursing home, her mother also lay down. She felt cold and embarrassed. She spoke urgently with God, asking for humility and patience. Then she had the idea that she should apologize to her daughter for still being alive. Her daughter had come for nothing. She remembered the story of little Hans who liked to cry that the wolf was there when it wasn't. She felt outrage at the thought that she might be compared to Hans. She immediately noticed that outrage was an inhibiting emotion for death. Was she no longer allowed to feel outrage? She finally lost patience. She struggled arduously against outrage. She was still tangled up in far too lively feelings. And then exhaustion washed over her again. She was too tired and too outraged to die. 'Exhaustion and outrage, I am withdrawing from you,' she murmured and lay in bed, trying to crush the ants with her back. Later, she sat at the table for a few hours. She lay her head in the nest of her thin, yellow arms. From there, she saw the trees growing out of the sky.

HIGH TIME

Tonight, a far-fetched woman is crossing a broad, brightly lit road bridge, over which a strong breeze blows. The sky is high above the Glatt shopping centre, warmth radiates from the tar, and the streetlamps shine soft lights onto the motorway beneath the bridge that leads into the distance, past sparse woods in which nocturnal animals are stirring. On this bridge, people realize that they aren't needed. The pillars stand regardless, and the cars seem to be driving themselves, the roads are tarred: they could fly off, right up through the air. In the Glatt shopping centre there's a button that opens the last door. But it's still there, that enormous, empty parking lot, where the far-fetched woman, in shorts, is now sitting in an open car boot, playing with a ball, back and forth, back and forth, the echoes reach the late customers in the Burger King. They've been waiting for it to be high time for a good while now.

WALDGARTEN

TWO NEIGHBOURS

Erwin, who is walking around in a shiny windbreaker and with a profound look, often feels that everyone is essentially like him. But since others are not actually like him, he sees that they have diverged from themselves. He finds it hard to know this and not act. Ideally, he would help everyone back to themselves. But how? Because they've diverged from themselves, they've also diverged from him and walk past independent of him. Erwin feels abandoned. But on the third floor there are two neighbours who take him as he is.

MAX

This summer, Max felt the need to reinvent
himself. He reinvented himself on a cruise ship.
He reinvented himself exactly as he was before.
But this time Max knew that he was the one
who'd invented him. And everyone agreed that
Max had finally found himself.

HUGO

Hugo was given a box of chocolates as a present. 'But I can't deal with these things,' Hugo said. Even though he said this, he was given a box of chocolates. He quickly ate one chocolate after another and said, 'I really can't deal with these things.' Hugo's visitor stroked his back as if he were a good horse, and Hugo grew very sad.

NEPOMUK'S JEALOUSY

Nepomuk has the trait of always reminding others of someone they once knew and loved. They come up to him and hug him. This happens all over the world. He doesn't know who that person might be. But he's certain it's not him. A profound jealousy begins to rage inside him.

BESIDE HERSELF

Melanie has a bad back. At night she is beside herself with pain. When she is beside herself with pain, she realizes that she's never truly beside herself. There's nothing but her.

ON THE BUS

Sabrina, who is sitting in the bus next to chubby Mark for the first time, initially can't believe what her friend Cindy is supposed to have said about her today at recess. But Mark, who otherwise says very little, has proof. He plays the recording of Cindy's voice. Clearly and explicitly, her voice comes from the device again and again. Mark strokes Sabrina's arm.

PACEMAKER

She wanted everything to finally grow quiet, but
then she heard the pacemaker. She hadn't
thought of it for a long time. She asked it to go
more softly or to give up the pace entirely
because she wanted to listen for death, which
was slowly approaching. The pacemaker said
that it couldn't do anything, that you had to wait
for the battery to run down. So she lay in bed,
exhausted, listening to the regular pacing in
place and didn't get any further. But then, early
in the morning, she was able to match its steps.
She walked at its pace through the halls, past the
rooms, through the picture gallery. She found an
opening in the wall and went into the forest.

AND FOR VRENELI

'Yes, for Vreneli,' Mrs Kramer said and from then on stayed at home on Thursdays. Before going to sleep, she added Vreneli to the list of those for whom she prayed. Last year Lydia, Gisela, Ernestina, and Ruth had also died. Mrs Kramer first prayed for Vreneli, then for Ruth, then for Ernestina, then for Gisela, then for Lydia, and then for all the rest, like Hedwig and Roswitha. At night, Mrs Kramer's legs ached and bit. She had to sit up and rinse off her blue legs before rubbing ointment onto them. Back in bed, she thought again of Vreneli, who had died two days earlier, just when she was about to put on her stockings. Mrs Kramer planned on more time for her visit to the graveyard on Sunday.

ECHO

Mrs Straub tries to face the accidents that will occur in the future by reacting to them in advance. It's as if she were pre-empting an echo in the hope that the sound that actually throws the echo will stay away because it has been replaced by the echo. As a result, she tries to fall now and again because a sprained ankle might dissuade the future from inflicting something worse on her. It would be implausible if, on the same day that she sprained her ankle, she were also to break her neck in some silly coincidence. But her fear of breaking her neck someday does not abate. In order to appease the future, Mrs Straub exposes herself to ever greater dangers. Recently, for example, she walked out onto a frozen pond to break her leg. She broke her neck there and died, with a sense of relief and of having anticipated the future.

PREVENTION

Mrs Gantenbein is able to thwart imminent threats by always putting glasses in the centre of the table or carrying the little bag that holds her wallet against her stomach. She also avoids clusters of people, darkness, and streets of the icy kind. Ever since she has been placing glasses in the centre of the table, not one of her glasses has broken and since she has been wearing her little bag against her stomach, nothing has been stolen from her. 'With my prevention tactics, I've always done well,' Mrs Gantenbein tells her friend Gertrude. Well, because she is hit by a falling branch in broad daylight, she immediately accepts responsibility. She should have known that walking under trees provokes falling branches. Mrs Gantenbein recognized and accepted her almost immediate death as punishment for her imprudence in time. At least, Gertrude hopes that she did.

LISA

When Lisa was twelve years old, she learned
that her mother was sick. She didn't know
exactly what that meant. Her mother looked
the same as she ever had, she was just more
noticeable. Something peculiar was at work in
her and growing. A few people suggested
guardedly that she might die soon. Others said
that her mother would certainly get better, Lisa
shouldn't give up hope and should be patient,
should summon patience however she could.
Lisa's mother had many fluttering friends in
baggy dresses and jumpers who went in and
out without ringing the doorbell. They would
stroke Lisa's head briefly in passing the way
you brush the first snow from a railing with
relish. A solemn sheen lay on the faces of her
mother's friends. 'My mother's illness
redounds to their honour,' Lisa thought and
was puzzled by this sentence. Her mother
followed several therapies. Each therapy

promised new hope and it wasn't clear to Lisa which held the hope, her mother or the therapy. Her mother had to take strong painkillers and had disconcerting dreams, which put her in difficult situations, which she nonetheless longed to return to. They made her feel as if she were being spun in wavering circles around a streetlamp. In these dreams, she could hear everything, the beating heart of a mouse, the crackling of a growing tree, the way lightning folded in on itself before flashing, and light tones like whales singing in the open sea. 'The whales missed turning left before England.' Lisa's mother had once read this sentence and it often returned to her since. She felt dizzy. She had the feeling that she was on a boat and had suddenly turned into a whale that was spinning around and drilling itself deeper and deeper in the water. Within this spiralling, she sensed fish and water near her ear and was enveloped in light tones that indicated places where she was to turn or where she was in danger of missing a turn. Then she would wake, look at her silent daughter sitting next to her bed, give her a nod, and fall right back asleep. This time she saw a peculiar little tree growing inside her, dividing and growing again. There was much growth and proliferation—all that was there before was supplanted, a fierce, disoriented capitalism must be running rampant in her, unchecked market forces going wild, and the invisible hand of the free market remained imperceptible, as did the market. Why should I sleep, she wondered and woke up. I also believe, I am confident, that I'll get better, she had long said to those who told her she should on no account lose hope because living had a lot to do with whether one wanted to stay alive or not. But then at one point, just when these friends were seated around her on uncomfortable chairs, some turning the flowers they had brought over in their hands, and outside everything trembled in the wind and clouds were being herded over the forest, she said: 'I'm dying. But how does one die? I have no idea how it goes.'

Her friends didn't know either. And they spent the time that followed in this ignorance, almost as if protecting it, huddled around it as around a small fire. Lisa was not part of this circle of friends. She couldn't have warmed herself at this fire, and when her mother died a few weeks later, Lisa could not believe it. She merely knew it. She didn't feel prepared. Wherever her mother had lain or stood earlier, there was now air. The friends who had come in and out before were no longer there. The smell in her mother's clothing faded. The sound of her voice remained in Lisa's memory, but it blended more and more with her own. A period began during which Lisa developed a slight hunchback, which she carried in the weeks immediately after her mother's death like a silent turtle that only occasionally sticks its head out for food or a quick glance at the world but most of the time remains in the dark, dwelling on what it has seen. Later, when Lisa was trying to slowly get rid of the hunchback through targeted and arduous exercises, she saw a bat shoot out of the nearby forest one summer evening. It swiftly circled a streetlamp and disappeared back into the rustling darkness that was softly spilling out of the forest like fur. For a moment, Lisa wanted to disappear into the forest, to be enveloped by this soft, stirring darkness. But then she thought of the cracking of the boughs, of the rustling and mysterious, nocturnal commotion of trembling leaves and dreaming birds, of paws on moss and coats of fur that rise and fall, that surrender their warmth to the damp ground and twitch in sleep, of ears that heard her steps before she even took them. Lisa looked to see if anyone was in sight, then bowed quickly before the streetlamp. Then she ran out of the light to her house, past all the mailboxes and ornamental plants, which she eyed with contempt and affection, and she decided to devote herself to her father who had until now kept his distance for reasons that were unknown to her and perhaps not very good. When she saw him through the window, sitting at his eternal desk, he seemed to be illuminated by the light of the streetlamp. Now much was possible.

HIGH TIME

Tonight, a far-fetched woman gets out at the underground tram station Waldgarten. A man carrying a flashlight and wearing a uniform a size too large gets in the elevator with her. Above her is the warm night. A Dachshund waddles past, the forest rustles and sways back and forth behind the house like an enormous pelt. The houses are flagged for demolition. During the day, he fishes in the lake and at night he wanders through the tunnel. Every night at exactly 1.31 a.m., when all the doors close, he sets off from Schwamendingerplatz. He always takes 35,000 steps but adds another 100 every night. The distance between the tram stops grows, the universe is expanding. He looks at his watch. 'It's high time,' he says and steps into the elevator. The door closes behind him.

SUCCULENT COLLECTION

ALBERT'S TIME

When Albert wakes and his daughter wishes him a happy eightieth birthday on the telephone, he sees the same trees and houses outside his window that he has always seen. But on this morning, it's the case that, Albert is suddenly absolutely certain, he has been gently driven away by time. 'I can only confirm it in retrospect,' he tells his daughter on the telephone. 'Because I'm always here, no one noticed. But keep this in mind when you come visit me.'

HOPE

You see him always harbouring hope. With a view of the lake. He harbours it with lots of ducks so that it has heft. If it were light, he couldn't bear it. But only when he can bear it does it give him weight. It's the only heft he can hope for.

LONG LIFE

Jacqueline decides not to contact him any more. The first day lasts an eternity, the second a week, the third a month, and the fourth an entire year. During this entire year, she doesn't hear from him. She assumes that after a year, it's all right to get in touch again and ask him how things are. She writes him and asks how he's doing and whether he'd like to meet at some point. 'Why not?' he replies. When they meet, she notices that he has remained far back in time. He missed an entire year. From this point on, for Jacqueline many long years pass in a short time. So that she can lift off into the future again right away, she wants to see him only every four days. When her friends ask how she's doing, she tells them, 'Somehow I've overtaken him.'

SHY

Amalia is familiar with the reproach that she's work-shy. But she clings to the fact that work is just as shy as she is. Work comes to her tentatively or not at all, and even when it does come, it disappears again immediately.

CLARITY

When Pauline lies on her back, she sees
autumn leaves like yellow fish on the skylight.
It's clear to her that these are yellow leaves, not
yellow fish. But what is even clearer to her is
that the yellow fish on the windowpane would
also be yellow leaves if yellow fish lay
twitching on the glass. From this kind of
clarity, Pauline later develops into a person to
whom everything is clear. No one can take this
clarity from her.

THE MAIN THING

Alice would like to travel along for a week in a foreign city. She could only come along, she was told, if she weighed this or that much. But she doesn't want to weigh this or that much. She wants to be as light as air. Actually, she doesn't want anyone to see her any more. And so, she would, in fact, rather not travel along on the class trip for a week in a foreign city. The main thing for her is to lose ever more weight. The main thing for her is to become ever more air. The main thing for her is for others to see her less. The main thing, others see, is for them to see less of her.

ELENA

When the old man with the walker approaches, stops at the fence, and gestures at Elena, who was reading in the meadow, to come to him, she stands up. He wants to hand the enormous binoculars to her over the fence so that she can watch the ducks as they disappear, one after the other, into the reeds. The strip of meadow on which Elena was just lying is a thin one. She wanted to read but it was suddenly indubitably clear to her that she couldn't read next to the sheep. The old man stroked Elena's bare stomach as she looked through the binoculars. When Elena takes a step back after a while and, thanking him, hands back the binoculars, he nods conspiratorially and slowly returns along the narrow path, leaning on his walker. Elena keeps reading. The sun feels too hot to her and the grass hard and rough. The sheep have lain down on the grass and are sleeping.

FRIDOLIN

Fridolin often sees things that astonish him.
For example, he's sitting on a comfortable chair
outside on a bustling square. While watching
different people, his eye is caught by a man
who forcefully reaches into the mass of
bicycles thickly clustered together in the
sunlight of the lively summer. With both arms,
the man grabs three or four bicycles, carries
them a few meters across the square and tosses
them into a large delivery van parked with its
doors wide open. No one notices the man and
the delivery van. He does his work vigorously,
disappearing briefly into the dark interior of
the van, reappearing briefly to grab the next
armful of bicycles, which he tosses into the
van. He doesn't whistle, but he knows what he
has to do and that gives him zest. The man
reminds Fridolin of his father who,
energetically and without reserve, would
gather up the children made lethargic by the

sun and bundle them into the hot car whether they were his children or not. The busy man goes back and forth between the bicycles and the van. His movements are neither rushed nor especially unhurried. He moves at a pace, in any case, that makes it hard to watch him. Even Fridolin has to search out the man anew each time he has to sneeze, which is often on this particular day. Then he looks at the man with astonishment. The man notices Fridolin's astonished look and returns the look, equally astonished and somewhat irritated. Without coming closer he calls to Fridolin in a loud voice: 'Well? Well? Do you want to call the police or what?'

The people around them glance at Fridolin with some distaste, then turn back to their conversations. The man grabs a few more bicycles with his huge arms, throws them into the van, locks the door, climbs into the driver's seat and slowly drives away.

THE VILLAGE

Anna, who comes from a flat region near the sea, now lives in a village. Mountain faces block the view. Light red apartment buildings stand in the valley like guardians. The firs on the slopes sway back and forth with eternal doubts. The sky clears only on rare days when the wind chases away scraps of clouds, slinking around them before dismembering them. Most days, however, the sky is misted over with all the breathing and hangs aspirated over the village. Anna's husband is in Germany for a training session. He massages feet. With her is their four-year-old, who speaks a clear High German. Anna goes shopping with the four-year-old. The child is named Tim and he takes chocolate bars from the bottom shelf. He piles one on top of the other into a tower. A man taps Anna threateningly on the shoulder and says something. Anna doesn't understand his dialect. She says, 'I beg your pardon,' in High

German and is appalled by her confident voice, her High German, her red fingernails, and the child, calmly building his tower. She can feel his suspicions hardening. She quickly puts the chocolate bars back on the shelf. A few of them are broken. They leave the shop in a hurry, without buying anything. She's moving so fast that Tim is almost flying, her straight back repelling the glances directed at her from inside the shop. It seems to her that they are punching shapes into the cold and when they're back in one of the light red apartment buildings, Anna turns the key twice in the lock. It sounds like swallowing twice. They play the telephone game. Anna telephones with Tim's foot. Suddenly, Anna's husband's voice comes out of the child's foot. He says that he's not coming back, he has fallen in love. Shocked, she lets Tim's little foot drop while Tim squeals with laughter.

THE LIGHTS

Outside, the rain made everything weak or
intensely cross hatched, then the sun came out
again, clouds drifted past or remained stationary
for a long time in thick, grey formations. Cars
drove by; people walked, waited, or did their
work; the world probably kept spinning—she
couldn't exactly see it through the distant
window, but she had the vague sense that it did.
A few times, Anna had visitors. 'So what kinds
of things are you doing?' they would ask
affectionately and indulgently. She was now a
child who was causing others worry, but once
there's a child, the worry is just part of it all.
'We'll manage,' they said, 'don't worry, we'll
find a solution.'

There were worries, solutions were found, a
replacement filled her position in the library
during her absence, letters and emails were sent,
bills paid, her apartment may even have been

cleaned, her mailbox, in any case, was emptied. Then spring came and she reappeared among the living. The trees bore round white spheres that one longed to sink one's face into, leaves had sprouted all around in a short period of time. They were ebullient and impatient and seemed to luxuriate in their impatience. They nodded in the wind and learned their first strange movements with the birds' feathers.

Anna noticed that she wasn't the same as before but had to cheerily show all the others that she was still there. People said that she now looked much older than her age and they tried to conceal a certain regret that wasn't free of reproach. The time before her accident now seemed to her like a clear, distant country that had driven her away without her ever being able to lose sight of it. Those who had always surrounded her were now bustling about animatedly and somewhat excessively still inhabited this land. She now inhabited it again too, although a few had realized that Anna's age, which now sometimes recalled one of those overgrown trees in the park that had always seemed rather absent and made them feel too loud and ephemeral, was an age they would never reach. They felt isolated and presumptuous in her presence but didn't let it show. For Anna, going on living now meant adapting to the living and to the standards of her country. She had to summon up every ounce of her will to do battle with the insurance companies, to regain the former velocity of her pace, and above all to forget or conceal the sea that had come between her and the land. Sometimes she succeeded, but then she was suddenly submerged in it again. Back then, just before everything was suddenly gone, she'd had the feeling she was being watched by the two headlights at night, she was already lying on the wet street or was falling, her bicycle in flight like an angular, metal moth towards the blinding light as if it were weightless. The headlights had caught her before everything went black. She longed for this illumination—or was it a gaze?—when she walked along the streets at night with slow steps and approached the lights. And because now, after the accident, she always seems to live lightly, before and after the country in which she simultaneously is, she has learned to cross the sea almost without a sound.

HIGH TIME

Tonight, a far-fetched woman is walking through
the city. A wind blows scraps of paper and beer
coasters her way. She leans forward as if she were
walking uphill. But she's walking along
Bahnhofstrasse, towards the lake, around the
metal garbage cans, around the ticket machines,
always bent forwards and under the gaze of the
store window mannequins. She passes groups of
swarming bankers and teenagers, moving down
the streets like stingrays. Above them the beer
coasters whirl, rubbing against each other. A
jangling spreads over the city and there are
gleams where the streetcar tracks run. The gold
lies far below, in uneasy dreams. The seagulls
have come, as have the foxes. Now rain sets in,
dripping from the gulls and from the foxes' fur,
and the grounds gleam too, the shadows follow at
her heels. She marks those places on the houses
where they will fold when they fly. She walks past
them, up the walls, always leaning slightly into

the wind. A loud rustling and the beating of wings will sound. Soon the time will have come. She has been anticipating it being high time for a good while now.